HAUNTIQUES

Raintree is an imprint of Capstone Global Library Limited, a company incorporated in England and Wales having its registered office at 264 Banbury Road, Oxford, OX2 7DY – Registered company number: 6695582

www.raintree.co.uk
myorders@raintree.co.uk

British Library Cataloguing in Publication Data
A full catalogue record for this book is available from the British Library.

Designed by Hilary Wacholz
Original Illustrations © Capstone Global Library Limited 2017
Illustrated by Rudy Faber
Production by Tori Abraham
Originated by Capstone Press
Printed and bound in China.

ISBN 978 1 4747 2550 7
20 19 18 17 16
10 9 8 7 6 5 4 3 2 1

HAUNTIQUES

PHANTOM'S FAVOURITE

written by Thomas Kingsley Troupe

illustrated by Rudy Faber

raintree

a Capstone company — publishers for children

1

Most people don't believe in ghosts or any of that supernatural stuff. So if I said that Stonewick is haunted, most people would probably never believe me. Regardless, things have been pretty creepy around town since the Markle twins and their parents moved to Stonewick from California a month ago.

The Markles bought Red's General Store, which had been boarded up for decades. They moved into the top half and turned the bottom into an antiques shop renamed Days Gone Buy.

Mr and Mrs Markle renovated the shop with the help of their twin daughters, Liz and Beth. Twins with pretty much the same name? Yeah, I know. It's confusing. We found out that Liz is short for Lizette, and Beth is short for Bethany. Anyway, the problem is, one of the items they sold from the shop, a hockey puck, had a ghost attached to it. My best friend, Hai Boon, and I saw the puck fly out of the window of his neighbour, Mr Preese. Twice.

When Mr Preese told us he bought the puck from Days Gone Buy, we took it back to see if the Markles knew what was going on. That's when we discovered that Beth Markle is able to sense spirits. We figured out what the deal was with that haunted hockey puck, and everything pretty much went back to normal.

Which is just the way I like it.

I guess I should mention one other thing. I sort of have a crush on Beth. Sure, it's a bit spooky that she can hear ghosts, but I don't care. She's a lot nicer, smarter and, well, cuter than the other girls at my school, all of whom I've known since pretty much forever.

I just wish I had the guts to talk with her about something other than ghost stuff, but I don't. So it makes sense that I wish we had another haunted item to investigate. As creepy as that is.

◆

"So are we going in or what?" Hai asks, crunching ice on the snow-packed pavement. "Hello? Casey?"

We're standing on the pavement across the street from Days Gone Buy, but I'm zoning out, just staring at the shop. If Beth sees me staring, she'll be pretty freaked out. I don't want to be creepy, so I snap out of it.

"Yeah," I say, nodding. I'm trying to muster courage. "Ready?"

We cross the street and step up onto the pavement in front of the shop.

"To be clear," Hai says, "we're here to look for a birthday present for your mum. Not because you want to see Beth, right?"

"Right," I say. I try to not let on that he's bugging me. If Hai knows he's under my skin, he'll never let up.

"But isn't your Mum's birthday in July?" Hai says. "And aren't we in the middle of January?"

"It's always good to plan ahead," I say.

"Uh-huh," Hai says.

As we approach the front door, I read the painted letters on the door's glass: *Red's General Store*. When the Markles fixed up the old place, they left the door as it was. Pretty cool, if you ask me. Before we cross the road, Mr Markle, Beth and Liz's dad, pushes the door open with his back. In his arms, he holds an extremely large box.

An older woman with glasses and a giant bun of blonde hair follows Mr Markle outside. She opens the back door of the fancy black car parked along the curb. "In the back, if you please," says the woman.

"No problem, Mrs Seashore," Mr Markle says with a smile. I can tell by the way he's moving that the box is super heavy and awkward. I stand there a second to watch since I have no idea how he's going to fit it into the

back seat. He pivots the box, slides it in and then carefully adjusts it. When he's done, it's delicately balanced so that the top isn't mashed up against the car's ceiling.

Mr Markle closes the door. "Thank you so much for your business," he says. "And enjoy your record player. It's a great piece."

"Yes," Mrs Seashore says. "It will look absolutely beautiful in my parlour."

Parlour? I wonder as Mrs Seashore gets into her car and drives off. In our house, we call it a living room.

When she's gone, Mr Markle turns around. He nods to Hai and me.

"Afternoon, boys," he says. He opens the front door as if to welcome us into the shop. "What brings you to Days Gone Buy?"

I need Mr Markle to like me, especially if I end up being Beth's boyfriend. If he ever decides I'm a loser, it's game over.

"Just trying to find a gift for my mum," I say. My stomach feels like it does when I drink too many fizzy drinks. "It's my mum's Beth-day . . . er, birthday coming up."

"Mate," Hai whispers. Out of the corner of my eye, I see him shaking his head.

"Well, poke around a bit, and let me know if you have any questions," Mr Markle replies. He walks over to the main counter, leaving Hai and me in the doorway. I don't think Mr Markle noticed my mess up.

"Very smooth, Willis," Hai says. "Beth-day? Oh, man. That's great."

"Quiet," I say.

I quickly check to see if Beth is around. She isn't. We wander over towards the dishes and teacups, but I'm not really interested in any of the stuff. I'm basically just keeping my eye out for Beth.

"Casey," Hai says from a display over near the front window. "Check out this old lunch box!"

Hai holds some beaten-up metal rectangle with pictures of cartoon cats or something on it. Directly to his right, Liz is sitting on a short, wooden stool, thumbing through a tattered old book.

"I guess we didn't scare you off the first time?" Liz asks, staring over at me.

"Scare us off?" I ask. "What do you mean by that?"

"The whole ghostly goalie business," Liz says. "Thought you would've had enough of our shop."

I shrug and walk over. If I can get on Liz's good side, maybe Beth will see I'm a good guy, too. "You guys have cool stuff," I say and mean it. "Even if you did end up selling a haunted hockey puck to a guy."

Liz flips through a couple pages in the book, which, close up, looks like some sort of notebook or ledger.

"Well, this would've been handy," Liz says, tapping a page in the book. "Could've saved us a whole lot of time."

"What do you mean?" I ask.

"I found this in the cellar with all of that guy Red's stuff," Liz says. "I don't know if he was a collector or a hoarder or what. But everything stored down there is catalogued in this notebook, including that old hockey puck."

Liz turns the book and holds it up, so I can see. Written in a messy scrawl in the middle of the page is an entry for the hockey puck. Another column shows the name of the puck's owner before Red got his hands on it.

"Gordon Williams," I whisper.

Liz smirks and spins the book back around.

"Maybe that was the only item in his collection that's haunted," Liz says. "But either way, if someone buys something, and it starts misbehaving, we'll know where to start."

I nod. I want to ask where Beth is but don't because that would mean I'd have to talk to her. Instead I say, "Well, if you guys ever need help with anything like that, let me know."

Liz stares at me pitifully, which isn't surprising. She probably thinks what I said was dumb.

"Yeah, okay," she says. "We'll let you know."

After pottering around in the shop for a while longer, I begin to doubt that I'll actually get to see Beth. She's probably upstairs in the living space above the shop, lighting up the room with her smile. I bet small birds come to her window and sing songs with her like they do for cartoon princesses.

"Casey," Hai says. "Can we go now?"

"What's the hurry?" I ask.

"Mate, we've been here for, like, forty-five minutes," Hai says. "I can't keep looking at the same junk any more. Besides, I've got a maths test tomorrow."

Truth is, I need to study, too. After a quick wave to Liz, we head out and walk towards our houses. I'm keeping quiet, thinking about Beth and being a chicken and all of that. As usual, Hai can read my mind.

"You have to stop being creepy," Hai says. "You're like a stalker, man."

At the corner of Spruce Street, I kick a chunk of snow into the street and watch it sink into an icy slush puddle. "I know, I know," I say. "I just get nervous and don't know what to say sometimes."

"Yeah, I get it," Hai says. "It doesn't help that Beth's kind of shy, too."

It's true, but it's also true that Beth and I talked freely to each other during our last ghost adventure. I can't explain it, but helping her help a ghost came naturally. When it comes to talking about regular stuff or whatever, I guess it's just a different story. "Okay," I say. I feel defeated and disappointed with myself. "I'll see you tomorrow, buddy. Maybe play some video games after school?"

"Sure," Hai said. "Unless Dad needs me at the restaurant tomorrow."

We say our goodbyes, and I head home.

I eat dinner with my parents and spend the rest of the night doing homework, which includes studying for my maths test. When I can't keep my eyes open any more, I climb into bed. Two minutes later, I slip out to turn on the light at my desk. I've been doing that ever since the ghostly hockey puck incident. Am I scared? Maybe. Whatever.

As I gaze up at the ceiling, I make a promise to myself. I vow that I'm going to at least say hi to Beth at school tomorrow. Or maybe Thursday or Friday.

Sometime next week for sure.

2

Remember how I said Beth is sort of spooky?
Well, she's not spooky like she'll give me
nightmares or whatever, but she is able to sense
things no one else can. It's . . . different.

So when I close my locker after third period
and find her standing at the locker next to me, I
jump. The Markles moved into town some time
before Christmas, and since they started the
school year late, their lockers are at the end of
the Year 7 row. Since my last name is Willis,
both she and Liz were assigned lockers close
to mine.

"Hi Casey," she says. She holds her books in her arms and blinks once behind her glasses. Not even her glasses can dull her eyes. They're like beautiful blue pools of water in a hot desert.

"Oh," I say. I stare at her eyes for longer than I should. "Hi. Hi, Beth."

She meets my gaze head on. I can't tell if she sees something from the beyond in there. "Liz said you and Hai stopped in at the shop yesterday," she says.

"Yeah," I say. My heart is doing dropkicks against my rib cage.

"She also said you'd like to help us out if there was ever any more trouble," Beth says. She glances over her shoulder before whispering, "You know, with a potentially haunted item from our shop."

"Oh, okay," I say, feeling my heart sink just the tiniest bit. "So –"

Beth nods. "We've got one."

◆

I can't exactly call it a first date, but Beth and I are on our way to Mrs Gladys Seashore's house. Even though it's still pretty cold, I've got a warm feeling inside walking alongside Beth.

Just the two of us.

All by ourselves.

Mrs Seashore's house is a large, older place with steps and a porch that wraps around the front. Ornate woodwork seems to decorate every corner. Even though I don't really know who she is, the name sounds familiar. Beth's dad heard she's a retired English teacher from the old school that closed down years ago.

"Didn't she buy that record player from you guys yesterday?" I ask.

"She did," Beth says. "She said it's acting really peculiar."

"So it's not just broken? "I say.

"Guess not," Beth says. One corner of her mouth frowns a bit, and it's beyond cute.

We climb the front steps, and Beth rings the doorbell. I hear the squeak of wooden floors inside as the footsteps get closer. A moment later, the door opens partway, and Mrs Seashore's no-nonsense face peeks out at us.

"Yes?" she says confusedly.

"Hello, Mrs Seashore," says Beth, displaying a heart-winning smile. "I'm Beth Markle from Days Gone Buy."

"My understanding was that Mr Markle would be along," says Mrs Seashore. She glares over the tops of her bifocals at me. "And who is this?"

The lady has creepy eyes. There's no other way to say it. They're the type of eyes that seem to bore right through a body. Also, one of her eyes doesn't follow in the same direction as the other one. I'm not going to lie. It really makes me nervous.

"I'm Beth's boyfriend," I say. Instantly, my chest heats up two thousand degrees, and my eyes feel like they're going to drop right out their sockets. *What did I just say?* "I mean, I'm just a boy. And Beth's friend. So, a boy that's also a friend. A friend boy."

Idiot! I scream inside my head.

"My dad thought we could take a peek and see if we could help," Beth says. She ignores the fact that I just uttered the dumbest thing ever. *Friend boy?*

Mrs Seashore doesn't look pleased. She probably doubts that a couple of Year 7 kids can do anything to help fix her record player.

"Please come in," she says finally. She opens the door fully to let us in from the cold. She doesn't offer to take our coats, so we keep them on. I'm sure she's hoping we'll leave right away.

I check out the inside of the house. It's like a museum with all kinds of expensive items all over the place. A massive, antique chandelier hangs over a well-polished dining room table with gaudy legs, the kind that has swirls on the tops and ends. Little cushions are built into the arms of the chairs, too. A giant cabinet filled

with old plates stands against the wall. I'll bet that crockery has never had a toasted sandwich on it.

She leads us deeper into the house, past an ornate staircase. "This way to the parlour," Mrs Seashore says.

Ooh, the parlour! I think and shake my head. We follow her through a hallway lined with intricately woven runner rugs to a big room with an old, shiny black piano in the centre. On a polished wooden table with decorative carvings along the edges is the antique record player I saw Mr Markle load into her car.

"It's this piece," Mrs Seashore says. She dabs at her bird-like nose with a tissue. "I have a number of records from back when I was younger that I'd hoped to play."

I've seen records before, but I have never in my life seen a record player like this. With a huge horn on top, the contraption seems more like a device used to let us know a storm is coming. *That's supposed to play music?* MP3 players are ten times easier to use. Seriously.

"I remember this," Beth says. She walks over to the record player. "Doesn't it work?"

"Worse than that, I'm afraid," says Mrs Seashore. "Watch."

We both stand back and watch the lady pull a record out of a paper sleeve and set it on the turntable. She turns a crank along the side, and I hear the gears and springs inside the wooden base wind up. When it's good and wound, she pushes a small button, and the turntable starts to spin.

Very carefully, Mrs Seashore sets the needle onto the record.

A scratchy noise pops through the horn, or speaker cone. I hear maybe a note and a half before something happens. The air changes somehow, feeling extra quiet or still. A second later, a chill runs along the back of my neck.

The arm raises itself back up, returns to the cradle and the turntable stops spinning.

"Is it supposed to do that?" I ask. I don't really know how record players work.

"Newer record players have mechanisms that lift the needle arm up, and the platter will stop spinning when the record is done," Mrs Seashore says. "This one is much older, though, so it shouldn't be doing that. It's incredibly strange." She strips off her bifocals to show she is seriously serious. "I never hear more than a second of music before it shuts itself down. And this is the third record I've tried."

"Did it play records back at Days Gone Buy?" I ask. I can't help but feel like some sort of detective.

"No," Mrs Seashore admits. "We didn't test it out. I saw that the crank worked and the turntable spun without problem. I even removed dust and lint from the needle."

I notice Beth suddenly seems a bit out of it. Though I've only known Beth for maybe a month and a half, I already know what that look means.

Something else is in the parlour with us.

3

Mrs Seashore stares at us like she expects us to fix her old record player. "It simply won't work," Mrs Seashore says, waving at the record player. "I paid a lot of money for the piece and was told by your father that this was in perfect working order."

Beth nods, but it doesn't seem like she's listening to the lady at all.

It's feeling more and more uncomfortable in the parlour, but I don't know what to say.

Elsewhere in the house, the phone rings.

"Excuse me a moment," Mrs Seashore says. She hurries off, leaving Beth and me alone.

Beth shakes her head and blinks a few times like she's some sort of scratched and skipping humanized DVD. It seems like Beth is listening to a voice that no one else can hear.

"So," I say. "What's happening?"

"She doesn't like that song," Beth says in a rushed whisper.

"What?" I ask. "Who doesn't? And how do you know?"

"I don't know," Beth says. She takes a deep breath and realigns her glasses on her nose. "It's just the feeling I got when Mrs Seashore played it. It felt like anger."

I glance towards the doorway Mrs Seashore took to answer the phone. I know we can't tell her the record player is haunted. She'll demand her money back and probably tell the rest of Stonewick that the Markle family, especially their daughter, is crazy.

"We need to fix this," Beth says. "She won't let go otherwise."

"So how do you know it's a she?" I ask. "Could you hear her voice?"

Beth nods slowly as if she's afraid of upsetting the ghost.

"Wow," I say. "Okay." I still can't get used to the idea that dead people can talk to the girl of my dreams.

When Mrs Seashore comes back, Beth surprises me and speaks up.

"Mrs Seashore, I'm sorry this record player is giving you so much trouble," Beth says. "If it's all right with you, Casey and I would like to take it back to the shop and see if we can figure out the problem."

Mrs Seashore dabs at her nose with the wad of tissue paper again and studies both of us. In a weird move, she pops the wad into the left cuff of her silk blouse as if she's hoping to use it again later. Gross.

"I was going to return it," Mrs Seashore says. "But if you think your father can fix it . . ."

"I'm pretty sure we can," Beth says and puts her hand on the wooden base. "Just give us a couple days."

"I'm having guests this weekend," Mrs Seashore says. She expels a drawn out sigh as she glances around the room. "I need it back by Saturday morning, otherwise I'll expect a prompt refund."

"Okay," Beth says.

Mrs Seashore glances at me, and I raise my eyebrows.

"Sure," I say, but I have no idea how we're going to do this.

◆

We carry the record player down the pavement. It irritates me that Mrs Seashore couldn't be bothered to give us a lift back to the shop. But, whatever. It's nice to be able to spend the extra time with Beth.

"So what did the ghost say?" I ask as we slowly make our way down the pavement. "Any clue what might help us help her?"

"It's hard to explain," Beth says. "When these spirits talk to me, I can't always make out words. This time it's just, like, a furious negative energy."

She readjusts her grip on the record player. I can tell it's not easy to get a good hold with her thick, purple mittens on.

"Do you think she's evil?"

"No," Beth says. "I just have this overwhelming sense that she's somehow protective of this record player. She seemed content until the music started playing."

I almost wish I'd looked at the record Mrs Seashore wanted to play. Maybe it was country, and the ghost just didn't like that type of music. I know I'd throw a fit if someone put some lousy songs on my MP3 player.

As we step off the curb, Beth slips and falls. She lets go of her end, and I'm not sure how, but I instinctively wrap both arms around the record player. I don't want this thing to fall and hit the pavement. Even so, it's heavy, and I wobble. My foot hits an icy patch, and I fall backwards, becoming a human cushion between the bulky box and the ground.

It hits me like a wrecking ball and knocks the wind out of me.

"Casey!" Beth cries. "Are you okay?"

"Yeah," I say from underneath the heavy antique. "I just . . . can't breathe."

"I'm sorry," Beth says. She quickly fixes her glasses and stands up. She reaches to lift her end of the record player off me. "I'm so clumsy sometimes."

"I get it," I say. I exhale quickly once my breathing feels close to normal again. "It's slippery, and you're from California. Not a lot of snow there, I'm sure."

"No snow at all," Beth says. "But even so, I'm a klutz. Not like Liz. She can keep her balance in an earthquake!"

Beth sets down the record player and reaches out to help me up. I grasp her hand, and immediately my heart kicks into hyperdrive. She helps me to my feet. Snow covers my trousers, but I don't even care.

Beth is holding my hand!

She lets go a second later and grabs onto the record player again. I quickly do the same, making sure we don't drop it just because I'm suddenly a little delirious.

"Is it okay?" I ask.

Everything seems like it's in the right spot to me, and the sound cone doesn't appear dented or anything because, really, that's all we'd need. We promised Mrs Seashore we'd fix it, so we can't end up smashing the strange-looking music box all over the icy pavement.

"I think so," Beth says. "Thanks for catching it, Casey."

"Anytime," I say. The winter sun has almost set as we continue on.

I honestly don't care what else happens today. I had Beth's hand in mine. Even if it was only for a few seconds, it was fantastic.

◆

We've finally made it to back to Days Gone Buy where Beth and I are carrying the record player into the back room. Mr and Mrs Markle are busy with customers, so they don't really notice us. Liz does, though, and follows us to the back room.

"So what's the deal with this old monster?" Liz asks. She already seems annoyed and has her hands on her hips.

"We think there's a spirit attached to it," Beth says as we set it onto the table.

"Perfect," Liz says. "Did you tell the lady no refunds?"

I say, "We said we'd try to fix it."

"Great," Liz says. She holds up the battered diary she'd found. "And this rubbish notebook is no help. I flipped through it while you guys were at that old lady's house. I didn't see a listing for this record player anywhere in here."

"So what does that mean?" asks Beth. She's watching the record player like she's bracing for something to happen. Maybe she's thinking something from the beyond might try and communicate with her again.

"It means that if this dumb record player came from the cellar, it's one of the few pieces of junk Red didn't log in his book," Liz says, flipping through the pages.

Beth's gazing off towards a corner of the room. Her eyes are empty, which makes me think something is up.

"Can you tell if the spirit is here?" I ask her.

Beth slowly shakes her head. "She's not here right now," she says in a whisper.

The haunted hockey puck was ice cold to the touch whenever the ghost was near, so I put

my hand on the record player. It's still cold, but doesn't feel frozen solid, like the puck did.

"Maybe we should try a different record," I say. "Are there any others in the shop?"

And suddenly, the table begins to rumble. My breath catches in my throat. The hairs on the back of my neck stand up, and I'm afraid to open my mouth again.

"Well, she's here now," says Beth. Her face is pinched and worried, but she's looking straight at me, like maybe I can help her.

◆

The table in the middle of the room finally stops rumbling.

"Okay," Liz says, a slight tremble in her voice. "What is *that* all about?"

Beth stands up and circles the table. She

puts her hand on the record player, and I do, too. Now it feels like someone left it in a walk-in freezer overnight. Within a minute, the temperature has completely changed. I'm surprised there aren't tiny flecks of frost on the polished wood.

"When Mrs Seashore tried to play a record, she didn't like it," Beth says.

"Maybe record girl doesn't want us to play *anything* on it," I say.

"First of all," Liz says, setting down Red's old diary, "I don't even want to know how you know this ghost is a girl. Second, are you serious? This ghost is picky about what music gets played? How are we ever supposed to sell this thing?"

I shrug.

"I don't know exactly what she wants," Beth says quietly.

"Well, I'm going to go and find a record," Liz says and heads for the door. As she does, I feel a chill rush past me. The door slams closed on its own, blocking Liz's way back into the shop. "Or, maybe not."

Someone knocks at the door. All three of us jump like we've been frightened.

"Girls? What's going on in there?"

The door jerks open to reveal Beth and Liz's mum.

"Why are we slamming doors?" she asks.

Before Liz, Beth, or I can explain, Mrs Markle walks over to the record player. "Your father said we sold that," she says. "What's it doing back here?"

Liz turns to glance back at the record player while Beth and I sit silently. "The lady said it didn't work," Liz explains. She glares at us like we should say something, too. "It wouldn't play her records."

Mrs Markle raises an eyebrow as she walks over to the antique. She turns the crank. When the mechanisms start to click, I half expect our lady ghost to do something. The turntable spins just fine.

Mrs Markle rotates the arm that holds the needle and inspects it closely. After a moment, she shakes her head. I can tell she's confused.

"This phonograph is working perfectly," Mrs Markle says.

"Wait a second," Liz says. "What did you call this, Mum?"

"I thought it was called a record player," Beth says.

"Phonograph, record player, it's basically the same thing," says Mrs Markle. "That's what they were called in the old days. Some phonographs were able to record as well as play sound. But not this one. The oldest ones date back to the late 1800s, but Thomas Edison invented the first phonograph that could play back what was recorded. I think that was back in 1877 or so."

I'm listening to Mrs Markle, but I really want to check the diary. I decide to hold off. I don't want to appear rude, especially if she ends up being my future mother-in-law.

"The interesting piece," Mrs Markle says, "is that Edison didn't invent his version of the phonograph to listen to music. He wanted to invent a way to record conversations to make sending telegrams easier."

"So it was like an old-school answering machine?" I ask.

"In a way," Mrs Markle says. "His earlier versions would make small marks in paper, like Morse code. Later, he figured out how to make the actual voice come through."

Mrs Markle pulls out a chair like she's going to sit and give us the entire history lesson. Before she can, Mr Markle calls for her, and she leaves to go and help a customer.

I thumb through the diary Liz found in the Days Gone Buy cellar. I'd peeked at it yesterday, but as I flip through the pages now, I'm amazed at all of the stuff Red took the time to catalogue in his old ledger.

I scan the first column where he'd jotted down a description of each item. I scan through listings for old books, a music box, an antique doll, a tool set, you name it. Page after page is filled with antiques he'd got his hands on. After maybe eight pages, I see a listing for a phonograph.

"Hey!" I shout. Beth and Liz come over to see what I had found.

"What is it?" Liz asks before I can even show them the entry.

PHONOGRAPH (crank style)..........Claudette Barnes – 232 Bridge Street

"Claudette?" Beth whispers. She says the name both as a question and as a statement. I wonder if the ghost responded but don't ask her. I'm too busy reading the address.

No way, I'm thinking.

"Maybe we should go to Claudette's house and see if maybe they know what to do," Liz says.

"There's no point," I say quickly. "Claudette's family doesn't live there any more."

"How do you know, Casey?" Beth asks.

"Because Hai's family does," I reply.

I knock on Hai's door.

"Hai," his younger sister Ling shouts over her shoulder. "It's Casey and two girls!"

The sound of footsteps on the stairs let us know Hai is coming. He elbows Ling out of the way and stands in the doorway. "Hey," Hai says. "What're you guys doing here?"

"We found another haunted antique at Days Gone Buy," I say. "There's an old record player that won't let anyone play any records on it."

Hai freezes. His shoulders twitch. "Well, that's creepy," he says.

"And we think the ghost used to live here, at your house," Liz says. She seems to enjoy delivering that informational nugget to Hai.

"Oh, that's even creepier," Hai says. He quickly glances over his shoulder. "But let's keep the ghost talk down, okay? My sisters already have a hard time sleeping through the night."

He lets us in, and we all sit in the living room. His sisters' toys are strewn everywhere, and a cartoon featuring sparkly rainbow ponies plays on the TV. Both Lan and Ling are sprawled on the sofas. They watch the show like little zombies. Neither of them laughs at anything the ponies say.

"So," I say, "does the name Claudette Barnes sound familiar?"

"Not really," Hai says. "Maybe my parents would know, but they're working right now. Even if she did live here way back when, what difference does that make?"

"I don't know," I say. "We're just trying to find out any information we can about her."

"Yeah," Hai says. "I don't think the previous owners left anything behind."

Beth's eyes dart around as if she's tracking a fly buzzing through the room. After a moment, she sighs lightly and seems less distracted. Liz looks at her like she just doesn't understand her twin sister.

"She's not here," Beth says. "But she was a long time ago."

"Okay," Hai says. "Don't do that spooky ghost-talking stuff in here."

"Maybe we should go to the library," I say. "We could see if Claudette is in an old yearbook or something, just like our ghostly goalie was."

"I'm in," Hai says. "Anything is better than watching the *Magical Mares Mare-a-thon*."

Hai gets up and disappears to let his two older brothers know he's leaving. In a few seconds, he's back and grabs his coat from the hook near the front door.

"Let's go," he says.

And with that, our entire ghost hunting team is back together again.

5

I pull open the door to Stonewick library. It squeaks on the hinges, but based on how empty the car park is, I'm pretty sure we're the only ones here. Well, except for Mrs Gulliver, the librarian.

Inside the library, it's dark and quiet. Overloaded trollies full of books wait to be shelved and stacks of books sit in piles up on the main desk. Mrs Gulliver sits at the main desk, fast asleep in her chair.

"Okay," I whisper to the rest of the crew. "We have to be really quiet this time."

"Well, no kidding," Liz says. "It's a library."

The last time the four of us were here, it got pretty crazy. We were here to find out who the hockey puck belonged to, and the ghost got really frustrated with us. Mrs Gulliver didn't see anything supernatural, but she asked us to come back another time when we weren't so loud and rowdy.

We slip through the aisles and past the stained glass windows that make the library feel like a church. We pass by the antiquated and rarely-used computer terminal that may or may not connect to the internet. We stop in the section where Mrs Gulliver pointed out all of the old yearbooks. I'd almost forgotten how many the library has.

"Okay," Liz says. "We're assuming Claudette went to school here, right?"

She's right. Just because she used to live in Hai's current house in Stonewick doesn't mean she spent her whole life in Stonewick. Even so, I think that searching the yearbooks is worth a try. The only problem is, we have no idea what years she might have gone to school. We know nothing about her.

I pull a couple of dusty yearbooks from the shelf and flip through them. Liz, Beth, and Hai do the same. Twelve yearbooks later, I'm completely frustrated. I don't see anyone named Claudette in any of the volumes I'm looking through. No one else is having any luck, either.

"There's something else we don't know," Beth says as she closes another yearbook.

"We have no idea if Claudette was married or anything. Even if we did find someone who we thought was her, she might have a different last name."

"This is dumb," Liz says. "Remind me why we even bothered coming here? It's not like finding her picture in a yearbook will tell us much about the record player."

I sigh and push away the stack of ancient yearbooks. Maybe it is a waste of time, but I don't hear anyone else coming up with any ideas. I try to justify my idea, saying, "I hoped that the students would have listed their favourite hobbies or quotes or songs beneath their pictures or whatever."

"Yeah," Hai says. "My cousin showed me his yearbook. Underneath his name it said that his favourite food was tacos."

"None of these have that, though," I say. "And I'm officially out of ideas. Maybe we'll never figure out what Claudette is trying to tell us."

A voice from the other side of the shelf, says, "Who are you trying to find?"

I glance at the others sitting at the table with me. Liz and Beth both stare back at me with surprised, identical eyes. Hai cranes his neck to see who just spoke.

I look over and see Mrs Gulliver walking around the shelf of cooking books. She has a small stack of books in her hand, as if she's slowly chipping away at the returns. Her eyes are staring over the top of her glasses at us. Small chains hang from the frames and circle her neck in case they decide to take a nose-dive.

"Sorry," I whisper. "We'll keep the noise down, Mrs Gulliver."

"You're being quiet enough," the librarian says. She waves me off with a small, liver-spotted hand. "I just thought I overheard a familiar name. One I hadn't heard in some time."

"Oh," Beth says. "We're searching for information on a lady who lived here a while back. We have an antique we think belonged to her, and we wanted to do some research on the history of the piece."

"And what was her name?" Mrs Gulliver asks. Her eyes narrow a bit behind her lenses.

"Claudette Barnes," I say quickly.

"Ah, yes," Mrs Gulliver says and sets the books down. "I knew Claudette."

"You did?" Hai asks. He seems more than a bit surprised. I remind myself that he's only lived in a small town like Stonewick for a few years. He forgets that everyone here knows everyone.

"Of course I knew her," Mrs Gulliver says with a bright smile. "She was my best friend, but she passed on quite a while ago."

◆

Mrs Gulliver sits down with us, and we tell her what we know. Truthfully, it isn't a whole lot. I'm afraid to mention ghosts or anything supernatural. Beth isn't.

"Mrs Gulliver," says Beth. "we're fairly certain that Claudette is somehow attached to an antique phonograph we sold from our antique shop. I think her spirit is clinging to it, anyway."

I'm shocked to see Mrs Gulliver nod as if she's not surprised by this revelation. She studies the stained glass window and smiles as if she's remembering something.

I ask, "Do you believe in ghosts?"

"I do," the librarian says with a slight smile.

"For how long?" I say. For some reason it's hard for me to imagine Mrs Gulliver as a youngster.

"I have since I was a young girl."

"But isn't it weird for a ghost to haunt some random antique?" Hai asks.

"It makes perfect sense to me," Mrs Gulliver says. "She loved that old record player."

"Phonograph," Liz says.

"Same difference, dear."

"Do you think she loved it so much that she wouldn't want anyone else to have it?" I ask. For some reason, I have a desperate desire to figure out why the ghost is still attached to it. And I really want to make sure we get it back to Mrs Seashore and keep the antique shop in business. If the Markles go out of business and move away . . .

"Claudette had a tough life," Mrs Gulliver says. "But music brought her endless joy. She loved her record player, which was passed down to her as a family heirloom. One could almost always find her listening to her favourite song."

I know we're getting somewhere. I can't help but get excited. "What song?" I ask. "Do you remember?" I sort of worried that I'm being too pushy, but everyone else seems eager for the answer, too.

"Oh, I've heard it so many times I'll never be able to forget it," Mrs Gulliver says. She's still staring off as if peering back in time. "It was 'Moonlight Romance' by a young man named Billy Sommers."

"Wow," Liz says sarcastically. "That sounds terrible." I wish Liz would turn on her filter.

"Well, at the time, it was quite popular," Mrs Gulliver says with a kind and gentle smile. She pauses and straightens her glasses. "Even though Claudette had Billy Sommers' entire album, she only played 'Moonlight Romance' over and over. Something in that song resonated with her."

I watch Hai pull out his smartphone. I don't even have to ask to know he's looking up the song or some titbits about Billy Sommers.

"Whatever happened to Claudette?" Beth asks. "Any reason why her spirit might still remain among the living?"

Mrs Gulliver draws in a deep breath before letting it out nice and slow.

"I have a pretty good idea," she says.

6

Once Mrs Gulliver collects her thoughts, she tells us more. "I grew up with Claudette, and we were truly the best of friends," she says. We went to school together and became inseparable when we were very young. As we grew older and began high school, we were interested in boys, dating, going to the cinema, teenager stuff."

The librarian traces the edge of a yearbook with her thin finger and eyes it as if she can remember the days.

"It wasn't easy for Claudette," Mrs Gulliver continues. "Many of the boys didn't like her. They thought she was ugly, as cruel as that sounds."

"That's awful," Beth whispers.

"Times were different back then. She always dreamed of getting married one day, of having a home of her own and raising a family," Mrs Gulliver says. "As everyone else seemed to find a perfect match, Claudette was left alone."

"But you were still friends with her, right?" I ask. "So at least you had each other."

Mrs Gulliver nods, and I hear her swallow hard.

"That's true," she says. "I was her friend until the end. But life sometimes gets in the way of friendships. As I got older, I became busy with my own life. I got married and raised our two sons. Those boys kept me very busy for years and years."

I think about Claudette, feeling like she doesn't have anyone, including friends who had time for her any more. Sometimes it's easy to forget about all the lonely people out there. Especially when I think about what my dad always says: *There's someone for everyone.*

"Being alone wasn't easy on Claudette. And to make matters worse, as she got older, her mind started to go," Mrs Gulliver says. "She was angry and claimed to see and hear things that weren't there."

"Sound familiar, Beth?" says Liz.

"Oh, be quiet," Beth says. "I'm not angry. Well, maybe at you for saying dumb things."

"It got pretty bad," Mrs Gulliver continues. "One morning she chased the postman down the street, screaming at him. She believed he was trying to hurt her when he was simply delivering the mail. After some other incidents where she nearly hurt others and herself, the authorities determined Claudette was no longer able to care for herself. They put her in an institution and kept her there. I visited when I could, but over time, she barely recognized me."

It sounds awful.

"So what ended up happening?" Liz asks in a not-very-Liz-like quiet voice.

Mrs Gulliver sighs and says, "Time moved on. The house she lived in and everything she owned was put up for auction and sold to help pay the bills. I suspect her beloved record player was sold, as well."

"Do you think she wants it back?" I ask. "I mean, it's not like she can take it with her."

Mrs Gulliver takes off her glasses for a moment and wipes a small smudge from one of the lenses. Her eyes moisten. "I'm not sure, dear," she says. "During one of my visits, when she didn't remember me, I talked about the time we spent as little girls. I mentioned the Billy Sommers song. I think hearing his name gave her a moment of clarity. Almost instantly, she told me she wished she could hear that old song again one last time . . ."

"On her old phonograph," I say, as if finishing Mrs Gulliver's story. "That's it. Maybe that's what Claudette's spirit needs to be at rest."

The library is quiet as Mrs Gulliver's story sinks in. It seems right to me.

"Okay," Hai says, holding up his phone. "It took some digging, but I think I found the song. Check out this album cover."

I lean over to see what Hai has found. A picture of an album cover features a young man with black, shiny hair holding an acoustic guitar. He's standing in front of an island background and smiling the most fake smile ever.

"That's Billy Sommers?" Liz says, hovering over my shoulder.

I turn the phone, so Mrs Gulliver can see.

The librarian nods. "Oh, that's him all right," she says. "I'll never forget the album cover or the song."

"Maybe we just need to play it," Liz says.

"Great idea," I say.

"I would," says Hai, "but it's, like, a dollar fifty to download."

I reach into my front pocket and pull out a two dollars. I slap it on the table like some outlaw cowboy at a saloon.

"I'll pay," I say. "And keep the change."

I sound a lot more "tough guy" than I mean to. Hai laughs and shakes his head at me.

As we wait for the song to download, I notice Beth has her glasses off and her eyes closed. She pinches her eyelids with her fingers as if she's getting a headache or something.

"Are you okay?" I ask.

"Yes," Beth says, with a quick sigh. "I don't feel Claudette here. I think she's back with the record player."

"Then let's get back there, so she can hear 'Moonlight Romance,'" I say. I stand up. "Thanks, Mrs Gulliver. We'll let you know what happens."

Mrs Gulliver eyeballs the pile of yearbooks on the table. Hai and Liz begin to gather them up to put them away.

"In retrospect, I wish I could've done more," Mrs Gulliver says. "Maybe I should've tried to buy the record player when it was on auction. Maybe I could've helped her find peace."

Beth and I stand still for a second. I don't know what to say. *Is Mrs Gulliver blaming herself for what happened to Claudette?*

There's no way she could have known that her best friend would become a ghost and then haunt the record player.

"I don't know if you can talk to her, but if she'll listen, please tell her I'm sorry," Mrs Gulliver says. Her eyes begin to fill, and she looks away.

"We will," Beth says. She touches the librarian's arm, and we leave.

◆

The song is downloaded onto Hai's phone long before we get back to Days Gone Buy. Hai begins to play Claudette's song as we walk in. Just a few guitar chords ring out from the micro speakers before Beth turns to him.

"You should wait," she says. "Let's wait for Claudette, and see if it'll work."

Hai nods and pauses the song on his music app. When Beth turns to lead us into the back room where the phonograph is waiting, Hai gives me a strange smirk. I shrug. Who are we to argue with a girl who understands ghosts better than any of us ever could?

After we walk into the small room behind the main counter of the shop, Liz closes the door behind us. Though she tends to act like nothing scares her, I know better. In our last ghostly adventure, she ran out of the library faster than I'd ever seen anyone move.

"Do we have to do this here?" Liz asks. She points up at the ceiling. "I mean, our house is right above us. What if Claudette gets angry and decides to haunt the place?"

Beth sits down at the table and places her hand on the phonograph. She recoils from it.

"Is it cold?" I ask. I now know that ghosts tend to leave cold spots whenever they're present in a room.

The room is silent, and the air feels heavier all of a sudden.

Beth nods. "Claudette is here. She's watching us."

It's no wonder I sleep with my desk light on at night. My skin tightens up, and I feel goosebumps through the sweatshirt and winter coat I'm wearing.

"Should I play it?" Hai asks, holding up his phone. He looks spooked. Blimey, we all do.

Beth takes a slow breath. "I don't know if she's ready," she whispers. "She's moving around the room, circling the table. But I don't know if it's excitement or fear or what."

"Play it," says Liz. "Let's get this over with."

Hai presses some button on his phone, and "Moonlight Romance" begins to play. The song starts out with an acoustic guitar strumming. The tune seems eerie, but I don't know if that's because I know it's the favourite of the ghost in the room with us or because it's from so long ago. The lyrics of "Moonlight Romance" begin.

Oh come with me, my darling dear. Take my hand, you've nothing to fear.

As the first few lines of the song play, Beth's eyes open wide. I can tell immediately that something is wrong.

Hai squirms as if someone just poked him. "Oh, no way!" he shouts. "Something just touched me!" His face shows fear, and he drops his phone.

"It's Claudette," says Beth. "She's not happy."

The song plays on. *I can feel you in my heart. Anytime that we're apart.*

Liz backs towards the door as if ready to run out the moment things get out of control. I hold my breath, not sure what to do or what is happening. Why is Claudette upset?

Beth is gazing around the room as if she can see someone here with us.

"She doesn't like this," Beth says. "Turn it off. Turn it off!"

Hai reaches down to grab his phone, but before he can touch it, it slides across the floor as if kicked by an invisible foot and disappears under the door near Liz. She jumps three feet into the air and shrieks.

"My phone!" Hai shouts. He stands up and runs for the door. As he does, the table shakes, jostling the phonograph.

"What was that?" says Liz. "What in the world is going on?"

Both Beth and I stand up and back away from our chairs.

"This isn't working!" Liz shouts. "Tell her we're sorry, Beth!"

Beth puts her hands over her mouth as if to hold back a scream. I have no idea what she is seeing or hearing, but my heart is galloping like a racehorse. I have the urge to run away and never come back.

"Claudette, we're . . . " Beth says, but her voice trails off. She nods twice and then stares at all of us.

"What?" Liz shouts over the rumbling of the table. "Stop being creepy and say something!"

"Inside," Beth whispers. She watches her sister with almost empty eyes. "The music is inside."

Inside? I wonder. *Inside what? Our heads? Hai's phone?*

Suddenly, the table stops shaking, and the atmosphere inside the room changes. It feels kind of like the air is moving again, not still and quiet like before.

"I have to find my phone," says Hai. He brushes past Liz and opens the door.

Liz follows him out. Clearly, she's happy for any excuse whatsoever to get out of the room and away from the ghost of Claudette and the haunted phonograph.

"That didn't work," Beth says.

When I look at her face, it shows a mixture of sadness and confusion. It's heartbreaking to see her like this.

"Yeah," I say. Since there isn't a whole lot else I *can* say.

"She didn't like hearing it like that," Beth says. She takes a deep breath and lets it out slowly and shakily. She brushes the hair from her face and stares at the old record player as if it might tell her something.

We spend the next half hour searching every inch of the shop for Hai's phone. I pick up the shop's land line and dial his number, hoping we'll hear it ring or vibrate somewhere. I search nooks and crannies. Nothing. Hai's phone is nowhere to be found.

After a while, Beth's mum calls out to the girls for dinner. I check the old wall clock. The shop is closed, and I need to get home. Hai reluctantly gives up. We both know it's no use and don't talk much as we walk back towards our houses. When he turns the corner to go down his street, he doesn't even say goodbye.

8

The next day I walk up to the front of the school where Hai waits along with the rest of the students for the doors to open.

"Hey," I say. "You mad at me or what?"

Hai breaks a chunk of ice free from the pavement. His dark hair blows in the wind since he refuses to wear a winter hat. He shakes his head and peers sideways at me.

"No," he says. "I was just mad about the phone. And scared. More than I want to admit."

"Scared of what?" I ask.

"Maybe we're messing with stuff we're not supposed to," says Hai. "This lady used to live in my house, and maybe now she's mad at me or something. What if she decides to haunt her old house?"

I have to admit, I didn't think about that.

"Did anything happen last night?" I ask. "I mean anything weird at your house?"

"No," Hai says and shakes his head again. "But I had to sleep with the hallway light on. I was so sure old Claudette would come and visit me last night."

I consider telling Hai about how I keep my light on at night, too, when the Markle twins come running through the crowd. Beth slips and almost falls, but Liz catches her by the arm to keep her from landing on her rear end.

"Hi, Hai," Liz says with a grin that makes me want to frown. Hai isn't pleased either.

"Yeah, funny," Hai says. "I haven't heard that one before."

"Lighten up," Liz says. "There's good news."

Beth reaches into her coat pocket and pulls out Hai's phone.

"Whoa," says Hai. He grabs it from her clenched mitten. "Where was it?"

"That's what's weird," Liz says before Beth can answer. "It was on the table next to the phonograph. Just sitting there."

Hai pauses. "She put it back there?" Hai asks. He turns the phone over, examining it.

"She must've," Beth says. "My parents didn't know anything about it."

Hai unlocks his phone, and after he checks it out for a second, he raises an eyebrow.

"What's wrong?" I ask. Both Beth and Liz stare at him, too.

"There's an audio file on here," Hai whispers.

"Well, yeah," I say. "Like, all your music?"

"No, Casey," Hai says. "Like a recording. Someone or something made a recording on my phone."

I feel a shudder all the way down to my bones. It's not like a shiver from being cold, even though it's cold enough in Stonewick this morning. This is different, like when you think there's someone standing in the corner of your room at night watching you while you're sleeping. A beyond creepy kind of shudder.

My ears ring, like they sometimes do when I wake up from a nightmare.

"This is just great," Hai says with a moan. "Now my phone is haunted! She jumped from the record player to my mobile phone. Perfect."

Beth shakes her head. "No," she says. "Claudette's not here."

Hai presses play on his phone to start the audio recording. He puts his ear to the tiny speaker at the bottom, so he can hear over the noisy students outside our school.

"Maybe not, but her voice is," he says, glancing at each of us.

I pull everyone further towards the street so we can hear, too. Hai restarts the audio and we huddle so close I can smell Beth's hair. Vanilla shampoo, maybe?

"Oh," Beth whispers. "She's singing."

It's true. Very faintly, I can hear a woman's voice singing in the background. The sound isn't great, like there's some static in the audio or something, but it is definitely a woman's voice that none of us can identify.

"She's singing that old song she likes," says Liz. "'Moonbeam Heartache,' or whatever."

"'Moonlight Romance,'" says Beth.

"Yeah," says Liz. "That one."

I have to stop listening. If I don't, there's no way I'll be able to concentrate at school or sleep at night. It's hard enough to focus on a Friday, but when you're hearing some phantom sing from the beyond . . .

"She's not going to let this go," Hai says. "What are we going to do?"

"Maybe we try to find the record," I say and follow it up with a quick shrug. I know it's better than nothing. Plus, I don't want to give up just yet.

"Yeah, yeah," Liz says and points at me. "Casey might be onto something. If that guy Red snapped up a load of old junk from the people around town here, maybe he got his hands on her records, too."

"Are you serious?" Hai says. Mercifully, he's turned off the recording of Claudette singing. "You think her records might've been in Days Gone Buy all this time?"

"When's the last time you saw our shop?" Liz says, arms crossed. "There's so much stuff in there, I don't even think my parents know everything we have."

"I still don't understand why the MP3 I downloaded didn't work," Hai says. I watch him pull up the music app on his phone. He presses the play function and then squints at a display on his phone's screen.

"What's wrong?" I ask.

"It says the Billy Sommers file is corrupt and unplayable," Hai says, holding up the phone so we can all see the error message. "Somehow, she messed up the song I bought."

"She didn't like hearing it that way," says Beth. "Maybe it just didn't sound right to her."

"Like listening to it on that phonograph is better?"Hai says.

The bell rings, and everyone streams into Stonewick Comprehensive School. As I head to my locker, I wonder if there's really any chance we'll be able to help Claudette's ghost. Maybe she just doesn't want anyone else to have the phonograph. I think about Mrs Seashore and how she'll probably just demand her money back. I'm trying to be optimistic, but it really feels like the record player is going to stay haunted, no matter what we do. Maybe some ghosts just can't be helped.

◆

I can't help it. I keep hearing the eerie, whispering voice of Claudette singing her favourite song.

They all say that love is blind. But I can feel your soul with mine.

I try to concentrate on Mrs Hennes' talking in class, but images of ghosts and record players keep popping into my head. I'm beginning to feel like maybe *I'm* haunted!

We all meet up outside school when our lessons are finished. After a short walk, we're heading into the front door of Days Gone Buy.

"I'll grab Red's diary and try to see if there are any records listed under Claudette's name," Liz says and zips through the aisles of the shop.

"The records we have for sale are over here," Beth says. She leads us past a shelf full of metal toys, a rusty wagon and racks and racks of yellowed magazines.

I'm not sure how I missed this before, but Days Gone Buy has a ton of old records for sale. There are so many that we each spread out and flip through a different rack of them. Most of the cardboard covers are worn out and faded from the years.

"Search for a cheesy-looking guy with a guitar," Hai says. "Good old Billy Sommers."

I check out each record in my stack before I start on the next one alongside Beth. She seems determined to find the album. She stares seriously at each cover for a long moment before she flips to the record behind it. Over and over and over again.

I hear Mr Markle assist a customer at the register when an awful thought crosses my mind: *What if the Markles had the Billy Sommers album but sold it already? Someone else in town or even someone visiting from out of town could already have it in their hands.*

"I'm not seeing anything by this guy," Hai says. "You think he was a one-hit wonder or something?"

Before I can answer, Liz is back with Red's diary. She has it open and is scanning the lists of entries that Red pencilled into the old book. All the while, she's shaking her head. "There's nothing else from Claudette's estate in here," Liz says. "I don't see any records on the list at all."

"So that saves us from having to pick through Red's collection downstairs," I say. "Another dead end."

"What are we going to do?" Beth asks. "Give up and refund Mrs Seashore's money?"

"Maybe we should give up," Hai says. "We're just going to keep making her mad. Unless she has another favourite song."

It doesn't seem like that's possible, given what Mrs Gulliver told us the day before. The song was "Moonlight Romance," and based on Claudette's anger over hearing the song on Hai's phone, it seemed she wanted to hear it played on her record player.

"Should we call the library?" I say. "Maybe Mrs Gulliver knows of another song Claudette might like."

Beth and Liz both shrug at the same time. Liz closes up Red's diary and nods.

"Might as well," Liz says. "Anything to get that phonograph and ghost out of here."

"She doesn't see herself as a ghost," Beth whispers. Her face is pale and serious.

"Oh, really?" Liz says, putting her hands on her hips. "What does she think she is then?"

"I don't know," Beth says. "Lost, maybe."

I wonder if Claudette's ghost is as confused now as she was when she was living. Maybe her spirit doesn't know her time in the land of the living is over.

Hai finds the number to the library on his phone. He dials and hands it to me. Before I can even argue and hand it back, Mrs Gulliver speaks on the other end.

"Good afternoon, Stonewick Library," she says in her kindly way.

"Hi, Mrs Gulliver," I say. "This is Casey Willis. We're still having trouble with the phonograph, and we're wondering if you know of any other songs that Claudette liked."

One of the shelves near us begins to rumble. A teacup teeters off of the plate it was sitting on and shatters. A wind-up, toy robot

takes two steps forward, and his light bulb eyes illuminate briefly. The floorboards beneath my feet tremble.

"I'm glad you called, Casey," Mrs Gulliver says. "If you bring the phonograph to the library, I might be able to help."

"Yeah, okay," I say. "We'll see you shortly." I disconnect the call and hand the phone back to Hai. As soon as I do, the rumbling stops.

"I don't think she wants to hear any other songs," Beth whispers. Her eyes flit around the shop.

"I think you're right," I say.

9

Having three other people help lug the phonograph to the library is an awful lot easier, especially with Liz there. She seems stronger than all of us put together.

"Do you think we should tell your parents they're selling haunted stuff?" I ask. We took the record player out of the back door before they could see us.

"No," Beth says quickly. "They won't like that."

"Who won't?" Hai asks. "Your parents?"

Beth pauses. "Yeah," she says finally.

I don't know if there's some sort of unspoken agreement between Beth and the ghosts, but I don't argue. If she thinks we need to keep the ghost stuff from her parents, there must be a good reason.

We get the phonograph inside the library and Mrs Gulliver clears a spot on the front desk where people check out their books.

"Put it up here, won't you?"

We lift the phonograph up and set it on the counter, careful not to bump it too hard. A haunted record player is probably even tougher to sell if it's damaged.

"Oh my," Mrs Gulliver says, putting her glasses on to take a better look. "That is

Claudette's pride and joy all right. My word, it's still beautiful."

Maybe I'm just not into antiques, but I find this strange record player anything but beautiful. Sure it's almost cool because it's old, but that big horn looks like a cartoon funnel for awful sound in my opinion.

"Do you think you could help us?" I ask.

"I'm hoping that if she's here, maybe I could talk to her," Mrs Gulliver says. "Or at least let her hear my voice."

Beth steps forward. "I'm not sure how or why, but I'm able to sometimes communicate with spirits," Beth says. "Maybe I'll be able to tell what she says to you."

Mrs Gulliver nods. "You're a sensitive," she says. "There are some people who are in tune with souls who linger in our world. I've read about others like you."

Beth bites her lip as if hearing that news gives her something to think about. "I need to learn what that means," she whispers.

"You have a gift," Mrs Gulliver says.

"It's more like a curse," Liz says. "She's always been a little different. Now this gift of hers just makes Beth spooky *and* different."

As soon as Liz finishes speaking, the giant unabridged dictionary at the end of the counter pops open and hundreds of pages flip past. All of us stop and watch the thick volume, our breaths held. I thought I'd eventually get used to seeing weird ghost stuff, but it's a reminder that the supernatural still keeps my desk lamp on at night.

"Did you do that?" Liz whispers. She's glaring at Beth.

"No," Beth says. "But maybe you should be nicer to me."

Mrs Gulliver raises her head to the space above us. I don't know if she thinks Claudette is floating around up on the ceiling or what.

Hai leans over to me. "You think I should record this?"

"Up to you," I say. "She doesn't seem to like your phone, though."

"Good point," Hai says. Even so, I see him open the video camera feature on his phone.

"Claudette," Mrs Gulliver calls. "It's me, Helen."

Beth glances around the library, distracted.

"We want to help you, Claudette," Mrs Gulliver says. She has her hands together like she's praying or something. "I know you miss your record player, and I'm sorry you weren't able to hear your favourite song."

The front desk where Mrs Gulliver usually sits to check books in and out, read and sometimes nap, begins to vibrate. The books she'd moved to the side shake, too. A few smaller paperbacks fall to the ground.

"Are you angry with me? I'm so sorry I wasn't a better friend to you," Mrs Gulliver says. "I know you had trouble and felt alone. I did the best I could."

Beth hugs herself and has her eyes squeezed shut. She shakes her head slightly. "She's not angry with you," Beth says. "But I think she's frustrated."

Mrs Gulliver smiles warmly as if glad to hear Claudette isn't mad at her. Even so, the counter continues to vibrate. I peek over at the phonograph, worried that the desk might shake so hard that the record player will fall and smash to pieces.

"Please, Claudette," Mrs Gulliver says. "Let us help you."

Liz backs up and bumps into Hai who is recording the whole scene with his phone. I think he's been holding his breath the whole time. I feel my stomach tighten and realize I probably haven't blinked in like five minutes.

"She's trying," Beth says quickly. "But it's stuck."

More and more books drop off of the counter. The phonograph is shaking, too. The record player's sound cone is wavering back and forth. If Claudette keeps it up, there isn't going to be anything left to bring back to Mrs Seashore.

I hear a small click and see a small section underneath the phonograph has popped open. If it weren't for the small legs on each corner of the record player's wooden base, I never would've noticed it.

And just like that, the shaking abruptly stops.

"What is that?" I say as I walk over to the phonograph. I peer underneath. There is something in the small gap between the counter and the record player. I reach my hand beneath and touch what feels like worn cardboard.

"What is it, Willis?" Hai asks. I know he's still recording, so I try not to say anything stupid.

I get my fingers on the cardboard and slide it out. I don't have to see more than the edge to know what it is.

"It's the Billy Sommers album," I say. I remove it from beneath the phonograph and hold it up. "Holy smokes. This is the one!"

"What?" Liz asks. "Was there a hidden panel underneath there or something?"

"I guess so," I say. I flip the album over to see if it lists the album's song list. "It's got 'Moonlight Romance' on here!"

"The music was inside," Beth says. She releases herself from her self-inflicted hug. "She was trying to tell us all along."

"Guess that explains all the shaking," Hai says. "She shook the record player so hard, the hidden panel popped open. I thought she was just mad about people messing with her phonograph!"

Mrs Gulliver claps her hands and then holds them in front of her face. "There's just one thing left to do, then," she says.

10

The Billy Sommers album seems so old and well-loved that I'm almost afraid to touch it. So I'm extra careful as I slide the paper sleeve out of the album cover.

"Don't drop it," says Liz.

The black record feels thicker than it looks but still sort of fragile. It's cold. Like walking into a freezer cold. That means Claudette is still with us. I set the record on the spindle very gently. "What now?" I say.

Mrs Gulliver comes over and gently turns the crank on the side. She pushes a metal button near the turntable, which begins to rotate. Then she tilts the needle and carefully places it upon the record.

The sound cone emits a few small cracks and pops.

"Here we go," Liz whispers.

The familiar guitar strums begin the song.

Mrs Gulliver puts her hands out as if she is dancing with someone. She has one hand up and the other on the back of her invisible partner. She closes her eyes and smiles.

Moonlight Romance. Last chance to dance.

Our librarian continues to whirl to the old song wafting through the empty library. She bumps into a nearby chair but keeps going.

I feel you in my heart. Anytime that we're apart.

A tear trickles down Beth's cheek. Is she able to feel what the spirit is feeling?

They say that love is blind. But I feel your soul with mine.

Hearing the word *soul* makes the hair on my arms prickle, though.

My darling, I feel you near. Come with me, and we'll disappear.

The words repeat a few times and there's a part where Billy just strums like crazy on the guitar. We're quiet until the song is over and Mrs Gulliver stops dancing. We all watch as the ghost lifts the needle off of the record.

"She's happy," Beth says.

Mrs Gulliver takes a deep breath. "So am I."

We're all quiet, just standing there. The air still feels charged.

"She's still here, isn't she?" I ask.

"Yes," Beth says.

"Wait," Liz says. "She won't let the phonograph go? What'll we tell Mrs Seashore?"

Mrs Gulliver walks around to the other side of the counter and digs for something hidden behind the desk. After a moment, she pulls her purse up and sets it near the phonograph.

"How much did Gladys pay for this record player?" she asks.

"I think it was three hundred dollars," Beth says. "It was one of our more expensive items."

"Here," Mrs Gulliver says. She pulls some notes from her purse. "Give her three hundred and fifty. Tell her you weren't able to fix it, and you're refunding the money, plus some extra for any inconvenience it has caused her."

"Oh," Beth says. "Mrs Gulliver you don't have to –"

"I *do* have to," the librarian says kindly. "It's something I should have done long ago."

Liz steps forward and takes the money. "Thanks," she says. "Thanks for doing that."

"No," Mrs Gulliver says. "Thank you. Now Claudette and I can spend time together again, like when we were young."

◆

Half an hour later, and we're walking away from Mrs Seashore's house. After apologizing that we couldn't get the old phonograph to work, Beth hands Mrs Seashore the money Mrs

Gulliver gave to us. She seems disappointed, but I think she's happy that we're being (mostly) honest with her.

"I still don't like the idea of refunding her money," Liz says as we walk down her front sidewalk. "But I guess it all worked out."

"Yeah," I say. "Seeing Mrs Gulliver dance like that was pretty cool. But sad, too."

"So you think Claudette is just going to hang around?" Hai asks.

"I guess so," I say. "Maybe that's really what she wanted all along. To hear her song and be with her best friend."

"When she's ready to go on, she will," Beth says. "When the time is right."

We walk a ways before anyone says anything else.

"You know," I say. "We're pretty good at this. This ghost hunting business."

Liz nods. "Yeah," she says. "But it still scares me like you wouldn't believe."

"Well, maybe that's the end of it," I say.

Liz shakes her head. "I don't know," she says. "We've got a whole diary full of old stuff that Red bought. The guy seemed to have a knack for buying haunted junk."

All of us are quiet. So far, Liz is right. Both the hockey puck and the phonograph were part of Red's collection.

"Maybe that's why he bought it," Beth says.

I shudder.

Is that why Red collected all that stuff in the first place?

SPOOKY SOUNDS

Most phonographs play records, but some early models were made to record audio. Back in 1915, Dr W. J. Crawford investigated séances and used a recording phonograph to capture the sessions. Dr Crawford was able to record light knocking and scraping sounds. Though he wasn't certain what he'd recorded was actually paranormal, it is believed Dr Crawford was one of the first to attempt to record supernatural voices and noises. Today, ghost hunters use digital recorders in order to capture EVP or Electronic Voice Phenomena.

ABOUT THE AUTHOR

Thomas Kingsley Troupe was afraid
of just about everything as a kid.
Now a full-fledged adult, he's become
fascinated by the creepy, the strange
and the unexplained. In his spare
time, he investigates ghostly activity with the Twin Cities
Paranormal Society. With his own ghost squad, he's stayed
in a few haunted places, including the Stanley Hotel in
Colorado, USA, and the Villisca Murder House in Iowa, USA.

ABOUT THE ILLUSTRATOR

Rudy-Jan Faber lives and works in the
beautiful town of Leeuwarden in the
Netherlands. Whenever Rudy has some
time to spare, he loves to lock himself
up in his attic and paint with oils. After
leaving his job as a concept artist at a gaming studio, Rudy
took up his passion for book illustration. He loves it when
he can make illustrations for super spooky stories . . . or for
stories with pirates or for super spooky stories with pirates.

GLOSSARY

acoustic guitar guitar that does not need to be plugged into an electronic amplifier

Electronic Voice Phenomena (EVP) sounds found on electronic recordings interpreted to be voices of spirits

heirloom valuable object owned by a family for many years and passed from one generation to the next

hoarder person who obsessively collects things

parlour room in a home that is used for coversation or hosting guests

phantom ghostly form displaying the human figure

phonograph old record player

séance meeting where people try to communicate with spirits of the dead

supernatural unable to be explained by science or the laws of nature

FURTHER INVESTIGATION

1. Hai finds out that Claudette, the ghost in this story, used to live in his house. Would finding that information scare you? Explain.

2. Casey and his friends haven't told Liz and Beth's parents about the haunted items they've sold. Why do you think they're keeping it secret?

3. Mrs Gulliver and Claudette were best friends for a long time. Do you have a best friend? Describe what kinds of things make two people get along so well.

4. Claudette fell in love with Billy Sommers' "Moonlight Romance" song. Is there a song with which you feel a strong connection? Why?

5. Whether you're musical or not, try to write a song. Consider making the lyrics romantic or having to do with young love.

Uncover the mysteries of
HAUNTIQUES...

HAUNTIQUES

GHOSTLY GOALIE

THOMAS KINGSLEY TROUPE

HAUNTIQUES

DARLING DOLL

THOMAS KINGSLEY TROUPE

HAUNTIQUES

WANDERING WAGON

THOMAS KINGSLEY TROUPE

HAUNTIQUES

PHANTOM'S FAVOURITE

THOMAS KINGSLEY TROUPE